生肖

To Marko Lijie Demosthenes

Snowfoxfables™

www.snowfoxfables.com

Text
N.I. Michael

The Great Race

The Story of the Chinese Zodiac

Illustrations

Persa Zacharia

中国

从前在中国古代

Once upon a time
in ancient China...

长城

Long before the Great Wall
was built...

The Jade Emperor was celebrating his birthday!
From all over China, people were sending him wonderful presents, delicious fruits, fragrant flowers, and much more... So pleased was the Emperor that he wanted to give them all a precious gift in return.
Until then there was no calendar, the years passed with no way to keep track of them and people found this quite confusing.

The good-hearted Emperor pondered how to help them.
He thought and thought, and suddenly an idea dawned
on him: he would hold a race. And not just any race, but
a Great Race among all the animals! The twelve winners
of the Race would each give their name to a year, in the
order they finished. And thus, a cycle of twelve years
would be established, with each year bearing the name
of an animal.

But what kind of contest should the Emperor declare that would test not only the animals' speed or stamina, but also their wits and teamwork? After reflecting on the matter, the wise Emperor found a worthy challenge. He decreed that the animals would have to cross a mighty river!

The news of the race spread
quickly throughout China:

HEAR YE

HEAR YE

玉皇大帝邀请动物

HIS AUGUST IMPERIAL MAJESTY,

THE JADE EMPEROR,

INVITES ALL ANIMALS

TO TAKE PART IN A GREAT RACE!

And so, the animals started
to prepare and gather from
far across the land.

熊猫

The Pandas were among the first to hear about the great event and were eager to give it a try. So they started practicing their special Panda swimming strokes. However, they got so tired from training that when they began to eat their favorite bamboo snacks, they forgot all about the race.

The towering elephants love crossing rivers and they too were at first keen to take part in the competition. But when they found out that rats would also be racing, they immediately decided to keep their distance. For they would rather dance on thin ice than have those tiny creatures scurrying around their feet.

And so it was that thirteen fearsome contenders finally
gathered at the start of the race, at the riverbank:
a mighty dragon with a gentle heart, a conniving, clumsy
cat, a graceful, swift-footed horse, a playful, fun-loving dog,
a ferocious, fearless tiger, an adventurous, inquisitive rooster,

ON YOUR MARKS!

GET SET!

GO!

a scaly, sneaky snake, a nimble, bouncy monkey, a sprightly, daring rabbit, a smug, cunning rat, a kind, burly ox, a meek, affable goat, and a plucky, sturdy pig.

THE GREAT RACE IS UNDER WAY!

How will each animal do?

猫、鼠和牛

The cat and the rat didn't know how to swim and were scared to cross the river. So they urgently looked around for a way to hitch a ride. Seeing the stocky ox, they asked if it could carry them on its back. The kind-hearted ox agreed, without suspecting that the two of them had a secret plan: the cat and the rat had made a pact that once carried safely across, they would make a dash ahead, leaving the ox behind and taking first place! The two rascals climbed upon the back of the benign bovine and held tight as it entered the water.

The strong ox rushed ahead, and soon the three animals were well ahead of the competition. But when the ox reached the deepest part of the river, the rat betrayed the cat and gave it a sudden push. The cat tumbled off the ox's back into the water and barely made it back to land. It took such a long time for it to recover from the shock that it had to withdraw from the race. And that is how cats became the sworn enemies of rats and mice!

When the ox reached the opposite shore, the wily rat said to it, "Thank you for the ride, I am truly much obliged," but then scurried ahead and snatched first place. The ox was stunned by the rat's audacity, but still it was glad to come in second.

Unlike the ox, the tiger did not go into the water from the shallows. Trusting in its powerful legs, it charged forward, and with one big leap reached the middle of the river with first place well in sight. It ran into rough waters though and struggled to swim against the waves. But it didn't give up, and fought ferociously until it reached the other side. When it came ashore, it ran so fast that it almost caught up with the rat and the ox. Thus, the tiger came a close third, saving the honor of the felines!

Although its speed was legendary, the rabbit was not fond of swimming. How would it make it across?

The rabbit took a moment to craft a plan. It scanned the river carefully and discovered that there were several rocks peeking through the water. By using them as springboards it could cross the river without so much as wetting its feet.

Without a moment to lose the rabbit started hopping from one rock to another. It stayed focused as it jumped onto the first rock then onto the next one, and it did not even think of taking a break – for the rabbit remembered well its race against the tortoise when it gave away victory by being overconfident and taking a nap! Alas, the last rock the rabbit was able to reach was so far from the shore that it couldn't hop from there without falling into the water.

And so, the poor rabbit was left stranded on the rock. When at last it saw a floating branch coming its way it quickly jumped on it. But the river currents changed and started pushing the branch farther and farther away from land. The rabbit had started to despair...

When a sudden gust of wind lifted it high into the air and catapulted it towards the shore! When it finally made it to dry land, the rest of the race was a piece of carrot-cake for a natural born runner like the rabbit. It reached the finish line swiftly and got fourth place.

Before the race began, everyone believed that the dragon would easily win because of its magical ability to fly. And yet the first four places were already taken, and the dragon had not yet appeared. What had happened?

While the ox had hardly reached the middle of the river, the dragon, flying mightily in the sky, was already nearing the finish line. But at that very moment ... A mysterious light far away in the horizon caught its attention.

Curious to find out what was going on, the dragon flew towards the flares and saw a huge fire threatening to engulf an entire village! The poor villagers were trying desperately to put out the flames. The noble dragon rushed to help them and with a deep breath blew the clouds in the sky in the direction of the village. Soon afterwards, a heavy rain poured on the village, the fire was put out, and the villagers were grateful to see their homes saved.

Once the flames had died out and villagers were all safe and sound, the dragon flew towards the river to resume the race. On its way back, from high up in the sky, it spotted the rabbit on the branch drifting away. Wishing to help it, the dragon took another breath and propelled rabbit and branch to land. And so, while the rabbit hopped to fourth place, the dragon finished behind it, coming in fifth.

The Emperor was perplexed and asked, "How is it that you, mighty dragon, a flying ace, only came in fifth in the Great Race?" But when the dragon explained what had kept it back, the Emperor was pleased and proud, and praised it for using its powers for good causes.

蛇 和 马

Back at the starting line, the snake took one look at the formidable line up. What was a reptile going to do against such competition? It got so discouraged that it thought of giving up and going back into hibernation. But then it came up with its own cunning plan: it would let another animal do the hard work for it. So it sneaked its way near the horse and coiled unnoticed around its left forehoof.

When the horse went into the water, the snake became worried that the fish swimming in the river would tell on it. So it kept telling them, "Sssssssss–hush, don't make a fuss!" And ever since that day snakes like to make a furtive ssssssss sound!

The horse crossed the river in great style and was about to gallop forwards towards the finish line when the snake uncoiled itself. The horse was so astonished that it froze. The snake grabbed the opportunity and slithered ahead. When the horse regained its poise, it was too late to overtake. And so, the snake took sixth place leaving the horse in seventh.

The rooster, who was an early bird, had gotten up before all the other animals and had been scouting the river for a spot where it would be easiest to cross. Instead, it found behind some bushes an abandoned raft. The rooster rushed to tell the goat and the monkey about its discovery, and they agreed to join forces.

The goat helped clear the twigs to free the raft and the monkey pulled it into the water, and, without further ado, the three of them sailed off.

Great storms and billows they encountered on their journey, but with the rooster as captain, the monkey as first mate, and the goat vigilant on the bridge, they managed to keep afloat and avoid all those rocks the rabbit had hopped on. And so, they made it safely across. With no bad feelings among them, the goat got eighth place, the monkey came in ninth, and the rooster tenth.

The rooster had scarcely finished the race when loud barking was heard in the distance. The Emperor and the animals turned to see the dog running towards them, all wet and out of breath. When it finally reached them, the dog started shaking the water off its coat, spattering everyone!

The Emperor was puzzled to see the dog taking eleventh position, for he knew that the canine was a great swimmer. So, he asked it, "What held you back?" The dog sat embarrassed before the Emperor with its tail between its legs. It confessed that when it saw the cool river waters it could not resist taking a bath. Then it got so excited barking at the fish that it lost track of time. When the dog spotted the rooster, the sheep, and the monkey sailing in their raft, it remembered there was a race under way. Mustering all its strength, it quickly swam across the river and made it to the finish line, barking non-stop.

Just as the Emperor was getting ready to declare the end of the Great Race, "Oink, oink, wait for me," shouted the pig. Confounded, the Emperor asked, "What happened? How is it that the swine was the very last to cross the finish line?" The pig explained that it could not run on an empty stomach. So when it discovered some irresistibly delectable truffles on the river's edge, it gobbled them all up. But after the feast, the pig was so full and drowsy, that it fell asleep. Fortunately, the dog's barks woke it up. Startled out of its slumbers and jumping into the water, the pig swam as fast as it could. It had a race to finish! When it managed to reach the shore though, all the other animals had already completed the race, leaving the pig in twelfth and last place.

故事结束

And so it was, against all odds, that the Great Race was won by the tiny rat and, in commemoration of its victory, the first year in the Chinese calendar was called the Year of the Rat. The second year was named the Year of the Ox, as the ox came in second, the third the Year of the Tiger, and so forth, with the twelfth and last year being named the Year of the Pig. The cat looked on from afar, disgruntled, but the other animals were pleased to have their names given to a calendar year. The people were grateful they could now measure time and the Jade Emperor was delighted with the success of his splendid idea. And so, the Great Race ended, and the counting of years began, with the names of the twelve winning animals, and continues to this very day.

Which year were you born in?
Find your zodiac animal!

YEAR OF THE RAT
1948, 1960, 1972, 1984,
1996, 2008, 2020

YEAR OF THE OX
1949, 1961, 1973, 1985, 1997,
2009, 2021

YEAR OF THE TIGER
1950, 1962, 1974, 1986,
1998, 2010, 2022

YEAR OF THE RABBIT
1951, 1963, 1975, 1987, 1999,
2011, 2023

YEAR OF THE DRAGON
1952, 1964, 1976, 1988,
2000, 2012, 2024

YEAR OF THE SNAKE
1953, 1965, 1977, 1989,
2001, 2013, 2025

Which year were you born in?
Find your zodiac animal!

YEAR OF THE HORSE
1954, 1966, 1978, 1990,
2002, 2014, 2026

YEAR OF THE GOAT
1955, 1967, 1979, 1991,
2003, 2015, 2027

YEAR OF THE MONKEY
1956, 1968, 1980, 1992,
2004, 2016, 2028

YEAR OF THE ROOSTER
1957, 1969, 1981, 1993,
2005, 2017, 2029

YEAR OF THE DOG
1958, 1970, 1982, 1994,
2006, 2018, 2030

YEAR OF THE PIG
1959, 1971, 1983, 1995,
2007, 2019, 2031

A glossary of Chinese characters used in the book

We would like to thank creative writers Marylle Goumas and Diana Farr Louis for their suggestions and Jane Ye for the Chinese calligraphy.

Note on the map of China
Darker shades indicate the areas in which Chinese civilization developed during the Neolithic period.

N.I. Michael, a '78 horse, is the creator of Snowfoxfables, a new series of illustrated children's books, inspired by world mythologies. For more information visit the website: www.snowfoxfables.com

Persa Zacharia was born in Athens in 1987, so her Chinese zodiac is the rabbit. She studied stage and costume design at the Department of Theatre Studies of the University of the Peloponnese and painting at Central Saint Martins in London. Her work has appeared both in personal and group exhibitions in London and Athens, where she lives and works as a painter and illustrator. She also teaches painting to children.

比赛